FURRY, FLUFFY & FABULOUS!

4 Pet-tacular Stories

By Amy Sky Koster

Illustrated by the Disney Storybook Art Team

A GOLDEN BOOK • NEW YORK

Copyright © 2014 Disney Enterprises, Inc. All rights reserved. Published in the United States by Golden Books, an imprint of Random House Children's Books, a division of Random House LLC, 1745 Broadway, New York, NY 10019, and in Canada by Random House of Canada Limited, Toronto, Penguin Random House Companies, in conjunction with Disney Enterprises, Inc. Golden Books, A Golden Book, A Big Golden Book, the G colophon, and the distinctive gold spine are registered trademarks of Random House LLC.
randomhouse.com/kids
ISBN 978-0-7364-3263-4
Printed in the United States of America
10 9 8 7 6 5 4 3 2 1

Pumpkin

A Puppy Fit for a Princess

Pumpkin loved to prance and twirl and leap. From the moment this little puppy was born, she wanted to attend royal balls and dance, dance, dance.

When the Prince wanted to choose a
puppy for Cinderella, Pumpkin knew she
was the perfect pet for the princess. The
dancing pup had to make sure the Prince
noticed her.

As the other puppies dozed nearby, Pumpkin stood on her hind legs. She twirled and danced, hopped and pranced. She wagged her furry tail and even did a puppy cha-cha.

The Prince knew Cinderella would love a puppy with such pizzazz. He took Pumpkin to the palace, gave her a sparkly tiara, and put her in a basket on the balcony. He wanted to surprise the princess at their anniversary ball that night.

Soon it was time for the ball. When the
music began, Pumpkin couldn't wait. She
was finally at her first royal ball! She hopped
out of the basket to stretch her dancing legs.

Cinderella had plenty to celebrate that night.

It had been a year since she had ridden in an enchanted carriage,

slid her foot into
a glass slipper,
and married
her prince.

All her dreams
had come true.

At the ball, Cinderella twirled, danced, dipped, and pranced until she and the Prince were alone on the dance floor. The night had been such fun. Cinderella couldn't imagine there was more to come!

The Prince asked Cinderella for a final dance beneath the stars. He took her hand and led her outside. As they walked onto the balcony, the Prince glanced at Pumpkin's basket—but it was empty! Where could the puppy have gone?

The Prince had no reason to worry. Pumpkin was just on the other side of the balcony, enjoying her own private royal ball. The graceful puppy was twirling and dancing, hopping and prancing. This was what she was born to do!

It took only a moment for Cinderella to notice the pretty little puppy. At first, the princess thought she was seeing something magical created by her fairy godmother. Then the Prince told her that Pumpkin was a real dancing puppy—and that she was an anniversary present. Cinderella was delighted!

Cinderella lifted Pumpkin into her arms and twirled around and around with her. She thanked the Prince for the most wonderful anniversary surprise ever.

Cinderella and Pumpkin have been together ever since, attending royal balls and dancing all night. Even on days when there isn't a ball, the princess and her prancing pup still make time to dance, dance, dance!

Teacup
A Performing Pup for Belle

Every day in the village square, Teacup the pup
performed for the villagers. She stood on her hind
legs and jumped about, hoping someone would
notice her. Teacup liked the applause, but what she
wanted even more was for someone to adopt her.

Some days she found it easy to shine—and was rewarded with treats! The villagers gave her biscuits and sweets to thank her for entertaining them.

Other days, it was hard for Teacup to shine.
The village streets were empty when the
rain poured down or the wind blew too hard.
Those were the days Teacup wished more
than ever for a home of her own.

One bright morning, Teacup was performing her signature move—standing on her hind legs while balancing a teacup on her head—when she saw a beautiful girl walk by. Teacup hoped the girl would stop and notice her.

The girl did stop to watch Teacup's act. That was when the pup realized it wasn't just any girl—it was Belle!

Teacup had seen the princess walking to and from the village bookstore many times before, but she had never had the pleasure of performing for her.

Just then, sunlight reflected off one of Belle's
golden earrings and shone into the peppy little
pup's eyes. The teacup on top of her head wobbled,
and then it toppled to the ground and broke.

The villagers were disappointed that the show was over so soon. They shook their heads in sympathy and slowly left Teacup alone. No one gave her any treats.

But the princess stayed. Belle knelt and picked up the broken pieces of the teacup. She gently patted Teacup's fur and gave the pup a warm smile.

"Don't worry, sweet little pup. I'll help you,"
said Belle.

Then the princess did something amazing,
something Teacup had always wished for: Belle
invited Teacup to live with her.

At Belle's castle, Teacup was treated like part of the royal family. The pup was presented with her teacup, perfectly repaired. And there were more yummy treats than she had ever seen!

Teacup had dreamed of being noticed and having a home to call her own. Now she's Belle's little star, performing for the princess . . .

. . . unless she's entertaining in the village square, where she always wears sunglasses to keep the bright light out of her eyes!

Berry

The Sweetest Bunny of Them All

Berry was a shy little bunny. There was only one thing she wasn't shy about—her love of blueberries! Berry would hop out of her cozy burrow anytime she smelled a fresh berry. That's how she got her sweet name.

It was a bright summer day and Berry's favorite time of year. The bushes were bursting with sweet, plump berries. Berry bounded out of bed to get a yummy breakfast!

That same day, Snow White and the Prince were strolling in the forest. They were also looking for sweet, plump berries. They were going to pick a bunch to bake into a pie for the Seven Dwarfs.

Snow White carefully selected berry after berry
and dropped each one into a silver pail. It was nearly
full when she came upon a bush with the biggest
blueberries of all. The princess knew these berries
would make her pie extra delicious.

But Berry wasn't going to let those big
blueberries go! Just as Snow White was
about to pluck a berry, there was a rustle in
the bush. The berry was gone! The princess
reached for another, and after another rustle,
that berry was gone, too!

Then Snow White caught sight of a fluffy tail as white as snow disappearing into the leaves. The princess loved all animals and wanted to meet the little critter that was taking her berries.

Snow White looked in her pail and found the plumpest berry. She placed it in her palm, knelt by the bush, and waited. Slowly, a little bunny with a berry-stained nose peeked out. Snow White smiled sweetly at Berry.

When Berry saw the princess holding that
big, beautiful berry, she no longer felt shy.
She hopped out of the bush, let Snow White
pet her—and, of course, let the princess feed
her more berries. Yum!

After one last stroke of Berry's soft fur, Snow White said good-bye. It was time for her and the Prince to head home to bake the pie. But Berry wanted more blueberries. She hopped after the princess and followed her all the way to the castle.

Imagine Snow White's surprise when she found Berry hiding in the berry pail! The princess laughed at the sight of the cute little bunny among the berries. Thankfully, there were enough blueberries for a pie— and for Berry, too.

Now Berry jumps out of bed every morning, excited to have breakfast with her princess. Snow White has a new treat for her bunny today: sweet mashed carrots! Yum!

Treasure

A Water-Loving Kitten for **Ariel**

Treasure loved the beach. She loved the smell of the sea air and the sound of the crashing waves. Every day she'd splash along the shore and dream of adventure.

Most cats are afraid of water and go out of their way to avoid it—but not Treasure. If there was a puddle in front of her, Treasure jumped in it!

Treasure was sweet and brave and playful. Most of all, she was curious!

One day, Treasure noticed a ship docked nearby. While the sailors were off gathering supplies for their next journey, Treasure quickly walked up the gangplank and stowed away on their ship.

Once aboard, this adventurous kitten dreamed of faraway lands and the riches she might find there. Treasure loved collecting beautiful trinkets of all shapes and sizes.

Treasure didn't know she was on Prince Eric's ship! Imagine the royal crew's surprise when they discovered a furry little stowaway.

Treasure was nervous at first, but the sailors were kind to the kitten, and they knew their captain wouldn't mind having more paws on deck.

In fact, Prince Eric was thrilled!

To Treasure's delight, the prince wanted to adopt her and sail the seas with her. The curious kitten with the shiny red fur reminded him of someone he loved very much.

And that special someone would be boarding the royal ship that day! As an official crew member, Treasure helped the sailors clean and decorate the ship for the occasion. As a trinket collector, Treasure enjoyed seeing all the lovely shells and sea plants.

As the prince led Princess Ariel aboard, a breeze blew through a string of seashells. Treasure loved the delicate tinkling melody the shells made as they clanged against each other. She leaped to paw at the shells, and the sound caught Ariel's attention.

Ariel picked up the kitten and cuddled her close. Treasure purred softly in the princess's arms. The kitten smelled of the ocean, which reminded Ariel of her undersea home and made her very happy.

When the ship returned to port,
Ariel asked Prince Eric if Treasure
could come home with her. Of course
he said yes. The happy kitten followed
Ariel to her palace.

The princess who was once a mermaid and the kitten who loves the water were made for each other!

Treasure is now Ariel's little treasure, and the two collect trinkets and swim together all day long.